Swept Away

A Krinar Story

Anna Zaires

♠ Mozaika Publications ♠

This is a work of fiction. Names, characters, places, and incidents are either the product of the author's imagination or are used fictitiously, and any resemblance to actual persons, living or dead, business establishments, events, or locales is purely coincidental.

Copyright © 2015 Anna Zaires and Dima Zales
www.annazaires.com

All rights reserved.

Except for use in a review, no part of this book may be reproduced, scanned, or distributed in any printed or electronic form without permission.

Published by Mozaika Publications, an imprint of Mozaika LLC.
www.mozaikallc.com

Cover by Najla Qamber Designs
www.najlaqamberdesigns.com

Edited by Mella Baxter

e-ISBN: 978-1-63142-129-7
Print ISBN: 978-1-63142-130-3

CHAPTER ONE

Greece, Third Century BC
2293 Years Before the Krinar Invasion

Her heart pounding, Delia watched the naked god emerge from the sea. Water droplets glistened on his bronzed skin, and his powerful muscles flexed as he strode out of the surf, impervious to the violent waves crashing onto the shore. It was as if the storm meant nothing to him—as if the sea itself was his domain.

Was he Poseidon? Delia had never believed the gods were flesh and blood, like in the stories, but she knew the stranger couldn't be a mortal man. The storm was raging, the wind howling outside her rocky shelter, yet the strongest waves couldn't seem to budge him from his path. Ignoring the battering of the deadly surf, he walked out onto the dry strip of beach below her cliff and stopped, raising his hand to push back the black hair plastered wetly to his forehead.

As he did so, he tilted his head back, and Delia saw his face. Her breath caught in her throat, and whatever doubts she had about his origins disappeared.

The stranger was inhumanly beautiful. Even with the clouds darkening the morning sky, she could see the flawless symmetry of his features. His jaw was strong, his lips sensuously curved, and his cheekbones high and noble. It was as if an artist's steady hand had molded his face, leaving no room for nature to add its imperfections.

With piercing dark eyes, straight black eyebrows, and a warrior's broad-shouldered build, the stranger made the most handsome men in Delia's village look like lepers.

A crack of thunder startled her, making her jump in her small, cramped cave. The man outside, however, remained calm, turning to look at the angry sea with what seemed to be interest rather than worry. Delia followed his gaze and saw something silvery shimmering far out in the water.

A ship? Several ships, perhaps? The object was certainly big enough—maybe even too big, given how visible it was from far away. Is that where the god-like man came from? That mysterious silvery something?

Thunder boomed again, and with a flash of lightning, the skies opened, sheets of rain coming down with savage force. Delia shrank deeper into her narrow cave, but it was too small to shelter her completely, and cold drops pelted her skin. Below her, the sea churned harder, the waves growing taller with each moment, and she fought the urge to scream at the stranger, to warn him to get to higher ground. She could see the swells rising in the distance; the waves would be taller than two men when they reached the shore, and the narrow strip of land where the man was standing would be completely swallowed up by the sea.

In fact, she realized with growing dread, her tiny cave at the top of the cliff might not be safe either. When she'd taken shelter here an hour ago, she hadn't counted on the storm becoming so violent. If the waves approaching the shore turned out to be as tall as she feared, they could reach the top of the cliff. She'd never witnessed the sea rising that high, but the old fishermen had told stories about surging waters, and she couldn't take the risk that they were true.

Coming to a decision, Delia scrambled out of the cave onto the rocky ledge below. Instantly, the rain soaked her dress, and a gust of wind nearly pushed her off the ledge.

Gasping, she managed to turn around. Bracing herself against the wind, she began to climb, determined to get away from the fury of the sea. She knew the stranger was somewhere below her, but she didn't dare look down. The rain was blinding. Even with lightning flashing every few seconds, she couldn't see farther than an arm's length in front of her, and her bare feet kept slipping on the wet rocks, her soaked dress tangling around her legs as she climbed with growing desperation.

Just a little more, she told herself. Another reach, another push, and she'd be at the top, on flat ground. With lightning striking everywhere, it was far from safe—Delia had hidden in the cave for a reason—but it was a smaller risk than drowning at this point. Squinting against the rain, she reached for the top outcropping, but instead of cold rock, her fingers encountered something warm—something that curled around her palm with unbelievable strength.

A man's hand.

Gasping, Delia opened her eyes wider, and through the blur of stinging rain, saw the stranger from the beach looking down at her.

The god had somehow made it up the cliff and was holding her hand.

CHAPTER TWO

The human girl seemed so shocked to see Arus above her that she froze, stopping her climb for a moment. Below her, a giant wave crashed into the cliff, spraying them both with salt water. There was an even bigger wave behind it, so Arus bent lower and grabbed the girl's other arm with his free hand.

"The water is going to reach here," he explained in her language, pulling her up as he rose to his feet. The wave was still cresting, so he swung the girl up into his arms and leapt back a dozen feet, holding her securely against his chest. A moment later, the wave hit the top of the cliff and spilled over, the water swirling around his ankles before receding back into the sea. Had the girl still been hanging over the cliff, it would've washed her away, possibly causing her to drown. Arus wasn't certain of that last outcome, but from what he'd seen of her kind, it was entirely likely.

For all their Krinar-like appearance, humans were weak and clumsy, unable to cope with the most basic challenges of their planet.

The girl began to struggle, and Arus realized he was still holding her against his chest. He loosened his grip enough to make sure she could breathe but didn't set her down. Instead, he studied her, noting her large brown eyes and smooth olive-toned complexion. She was young; he guessed her age to be somewhere in the late teens or early twenties. With her thick dark hair and slender build, she could almost pass for a Krinar female—except her features were too irregular to have been designed in a lab. Her face was shaped like a heart, with a forehead that was a shade too wide and a mouth that was too delicate for true beauty. Still, she was pretty in a unique way.

Pretty enough that his cock stirred, oblivious to the cold water pouring from the sky.

As if sensing the direction of his thoughts, the girl redoubled her efforts to get free. "Please, let me go."

Her voice held a note of fear, and her small hands pushed at his chest, her palms sliding on his wet skin.

To his shock, Arus felt heat streaking down his spine at her touch, and his breathing picked up.

He was getting turned on by a wet, scared human girl.

Before he could decide what to do about that, he saw another wave cresting over the cliff. The worst of the storm surge had yet to come, which meant his first priority was getting the girl to safety.

"We have to get away from this beach," he told her, turning away from the sea. She continued to struggle, but he ignored it, holding her tightly as he walked toward the hills in the distance. He knew there was a village to the west—likely the girl's village—so he headed east, where he would be less likely to run into more humans.

He was supposed to observe the Earth's residents, not interact with them.

Still, Arus wasn't sorry he'd saved the girl. The more he thought about it, the more convinced he became that she would've drowned on her own. And that would've been a shame, because she was pleasant to hold.

So pleasant, in fact, that he couldn't help imagining how it would feel if he held her underneath him, his cock buried in her slick, warm flesh.

"Where are you taking me?" The girl sounded panicked now. "Please, I have to get home."

"Don't worry. I won't hurt you." Arus glanced down at his captive. Her rapid pulse was visible at the base of her throat, and his arousal grew as he imagined the coppery taste of her blood on his tongue. He had tried drinking human blood once before, and the experience had been sublime. He had a feeling that with this girl, it would be even better.

It seemed that his decision was already made.

"Where are you taking me?" the girl asked again, her voice shaking. She didn't seem the least bit soothed by Arus's reassurance.

"I'm taking you someplace you'll be warm and safe." Surely she would appreciate that. He could feel her shivering; the rough rag that served as her dress was soaked and had to be chilling her. "You shouldn't be out in this storm," he added when jagged lightning cut across the sky for the third time in as many seconds.

"I'll be fine if you let me go." Pushing at his chest again, the girl tried to twist out of his hold. "Please, let me down."

Arus sighed and picked up his pace, ignoring her puny struggles. Once he got her warm and dry, he'll work on calming her down.

He didn't want her frightened in his bed.

CHAPTER THREE

Delia had never been so frightened in her life. The god—and she was now sure he was a god—was carrying her without any sign of tiring, his arms like iron bands around her back and knees. Neither rain nor wind seemed to slow him down; holding her against his chest, he was walking faster than a mortal man could run.

"Please, let me down," she begged again, pushing at his broad chest. It was useless, like trying to move a mountain. "Please, I'll sacrifice a goat in your honor if you let me go."

That seemed to get his attention. "A goat?" He looked down at her as he kept walking. "Why would I want that?"

Delia's breath hitched at the intensity of his gaze. "Because you're a god?" Despite her certainty, her words came out as a question, and she silently berated herself for sounding foolish. "I mean, because you're a god and deserve to be respected," she said in a firmer tone.

There, that was better. Surely he would accept one goat. Her family couldn't spare more—even one would leave them without enough cheese for trading.

To her surprise, the stranger laughed, the sound deep and genuinely amused. "A god?" His dark eyes gleamed as another bolt of lightning split the sky above them. "You think I'm a god?"

Delia blinked the rain out of her eyes. "Are you saying you're not?"

He laughed again, the sound blending with a boom of thunder, and she felt his pace accelerate from a walk to a run. He was moving so fast the ground looked like a blur under his feet. Delia began to feel nauseated but didn't dare close her eyes.

She had to see where he was taking her.

After a few minutes, she realized he was heading for the hills to the east of her village. There was a forest there. Maybe he hoped to find shelter under the trees? She knew trees were dangerous during lightning storms, but maybe they weren't dangerous for him.

Maybe he was as impervious to Zeus's fury as he was to the waves in the sea.

What did he intend with her? Delia's stomach churned, and she knew it was as much from her anxiety as her captor's running speed. The god had said she would be warm and safe, but he was taking her away from her village—away from her family and people who could help her. Delia's sisters had to be worried already. Eugenia, the oldest, had noticed the darkening sky this morning and told her not to go searching for mussels, but Delia had been determined to gather extra food for their dinner tonight. With five daughters to feed, her family was always struggling, and Delia tried to help as much as she could.

Well, as much as she could without marrying the blacksmith, who'd begun courting her after his wife's death last month.

"You should accept Phanias," Delia's mother had told her two weeks ago. "I know you don't like the man, but he's a good provider."

He was also old, fat, and had beaten his last wife, but Delia hadn't bothered pointing that out. Her mother didn't care about such minor things. Her only concern was having enough food on the table, and she believed that Delia—the prettiest of her grown daughters—was the key to achieving that goal. Delia had been trying to delay the inevitable, but she knew it was only a matter of time before her father gave in to her mother's urgings and made Delia accept Phanias's offer.

"Here we are," the god said, startling her out of her thoughts, and Delia saw that they were already at the forest. Stopping under a thick tree, he lowered her to her feet. "We should be far enough from the storm surge now."

He was still holding her, his large hands gripping her waist, and Delia's breathing turned uneven as she tilted her head back to meet his dark gaze. She was one of the tallest women in her village, but the stranger was much taller. With both of them standing, the top of her head only came up to his chin, and his naked body was powerfully muscled.

To her amazement, Delia realized fear wasn't the only thing she was feeling. There was a strange melting sensation in her core, a pooling of heat that made her pulse throb and her insides ache in an odd way.

"Why did you bring me here?" She tried to keep her voice steady as she pushed at his chest again. His flesh was hard under her fingers, his skin smooth and warm to the touch. Even through her soaked dress, she could feel the heat of his palms where he gripped her, and the unfamiliar ache within her intensified. "What do you want from me?"

To her relief, the god released her and stepped back. "Right now, I want us both to get dry and warm." His voice sounded strained, as if he were in pain. Before Delia could wonder about that, her gaze landed on his lower body, and her breath stuttered in shock.

The stranger was fully aroused, his erection hard and massive as it curved up toward his flat, ridged stomach.

Gasping, Delia took a step back, but he was already turning away from her. Extending one powerful arm in front of him, he said something in a foreign language, and she saw that he was wearing a silvery band around his wrist. She opened her mouth to ask him about that, but before she could utter a word, she heard a low humming noise—almost like a buzzing of a thousand tiny insects.

Startled, Delia looked up at the tree, but the buzzing wasn't coming from there. The sound was emanating from somewhere in front of the stranger.

"Don't be afraid," he said, turning to face her again, and her eyes widened as she saw the air behind him begin to shimmer. The shimmer intensified, brightening with each second, and then she saw a transparent bubble rising behind him—a structure that looked like a mushroom cap made out of water.

"It's a tool I have, not magic," he said, watching her, but Delia knew he had to be lying. Her knees began to shake, and she backed away instinctively, afraid the bubble would swallow her as it grew. The wet bark of the tree pressed against her back, stopping her, and she turned to run, determined to get away from the god with such frightening powers.

Before she could take more than two steps, his steely fingers closed around her arm, turning her around. "Don't be afraid," he repeated, holding her, and she saw that the bubble behind him was no longer moving. It was now taller than him and wide enough to fit five people.

"W-what is that?" Her teeth chattered, and she had no idea if it was from shock or the cold rain and wind. "H-how did you—"

"Shh, it's all right. Let's go inside and get you warm." Wrapping one muscular arm around her shoulders, he pulled her against his side and shepherded her toward the magical structure. "It won't hurt you."

Delia tried to dig in her heels, but it was futile. She could no more resist his strength than she could fight a rip current. Within a moment, he had her standing in front of the water-like wall—a part of which disintegrated as they approached, creating a sizable opening.

Delia froze with pure terror, but he was already leading her through the opening. As soon as they stepped inside, she realized there was no more rain or wind.

They were shielded by the bubble the god had created.

CHAPTER FOUR

The human girl was shaking so hard Arus thought she might pass out. He hated terrifying her like this, but he didn't know any other way to get her out of the storm quickly. Her skin felt chilled as he held her pressed against his side, and he had no doubt the poor thing was cold.

Cold and scared of technology she couldn't possibly understand.

Loosening his grip on her, Arus let her twist out of his embrace. It probably didn't help that he was naked and hard, he thought wryly. He'd heard her gasp when her eyes landed on his erection earlier, and he had no doubt the evidence of his desire added to her nervousness. He had to calm her down, but first, he needed to make sure her health wouldn't suffer from this storm.

His computer was on his left wrist, so Arus lifted his arm and commanded, "Set the temperature to human comfort level."

He spoke in Krinar, and he could see the girl turning pale as the nanomachines went to work again, speeding up the air molecules around them to create warmth. He wished he could explain about force-field technology and microwaves, but her people knew so little about science that it would take him months to teach her just the basics.

"I'm not going to hurt you," he repeated instead, speaking her language. She didn't look the least bit reassured, her eyes wide and panicky as she stared at him, and he realized there was nothing he could say to calm her down.

He'd have to come up with another way to soothe her.

Stepping toward the girl, Arus picked her up and sat down on the ground, holding her on his lap. She stiffened immediately, her hands pushing at him again, but he kept his grip gentle and nonthreatening, hoping she'd settle down when she saw he meant her no harm.

"Everything is fine. You have nothing to fear," he told her softly, stroking her hair as she kept trying to wriggle out of his hold. The feel of her ass moving on his lap was arousing him further, which wasn't helping matters. Thankfully, after a couple of minutes, she seemed to exhaust herself and her struggles eased, letting him settle her more comfortably against him.

"I'm Arus," he said when she stilled completely and stared up at him, her chest heaving with rapid breathing. "What's your name?"

"Ares?" She tensed, her eyes growing wide again. "You're the god of war?"

"No. Ar-us, not Ar-es." He repeated his name slower, letting her hear the difference. "I'm not the god of war, I promise you."

Her slender throat moved as she swallowed. "What kind of god are you, then?"

"I'm not a god," Arus said patiently. "I'm just a visitor from far away. Where I live, everybody can do what I do."

She stared at him, and Arus knew she didn't believe him. Rather than waste energy trying to convince her, he asked again, "What's your name?"

The girl licked her lips in a nervous gesture. "I'm Delia."

"Delia." Good. They were making progress. "Are you from nearby, Delia?"

She nodded, still looking wary. "My village is to the east."

"Right, I thought so." Arus kept his tone casual despite his growing hunger. He couldn't see much of her body under her shapeless dress, but he could feel its soft, slender curves, and his gaze kept drifting down to the throbbing pulse at the base of her throat. Now that they were out of the rain, he could smell her delicate feminine scent, and his mouth watered as he imagined tasting her all over. With effort, he wrenched his thoughts away from sex. "What made you come out in the storm today?" he asked, forcing himself to carry on the conversation that seemed to be calming her.

"I wanted to gather some mussels." The girl—Delia—shifted on his lap, and he knew she had to feel his erection pressing into her ass. It didn't seem to frighten her as much as his technology, and Arus realized he'd done the right thing by using his embrace to calm her. The best way to demonstrate his nonviolent intent was to hold her and let her get used to his touch, so she'd stop fearing it.

So she'd focus on him as a man, rather than a stranger with magical powers.

"Are you hungry?" he asked, resuming stroking her hair. Even damp from the rain, it felt thick and silky to the touch. "Is that why you had to go out in this weather?"

She blinked up at him. "No, I just always gather mussels in the morning. My family needs the extra food."

"I see." He'd already guessed that she was poor. Even by human standards, her roughly made clothes were quite primitive. "So your family sent you out in this weather?"

"No, my sister warned me against going, but I thought the storm wouldn't be this bad."

Of course. Arus had forgotten that her people didn't have a way to track the storm and measure its strength. All they had to go on was the weather at the present moment and whatever experience their elderly had gathered over their short lifespans.

"Well, you're safe now," he told the girl, whose shaking was finally subsiding. Outside, the storm raged on, but inside their shelter, the temperature was comfortably warm. "Nothing can hurt you here."

She looked up at the transparent bubble over their heads, and he realized how odd the force-shield walls had to appear to her. When she met his gaze again, he wasn't the least bit surprised to hear her ask,

"What are you? Where do you come from, if not Mount Olympus?"

"I come from another world, a planet similar to this one," Arus said, though he knew the girl wouldn't understand. "It's very far from here."

"Another world?" He felt a tremor go through her. "Like Hades?"

"No, not like Hades." Arus stroked her back in a calming motion. "It's beautiful where I live. Very green and bright."

She gave him a puzzled look. "Why are you here then?"

"Because I wanted to see your planet," Arus said, watching her lips. For some reason, that imperfect, delicate mouth of hers kept drawing his attention. "Your people fascinate me."

"We do?" Her tongue came out to wet her lips, the gesture unconsciously seductive, and Arus felt his hunger intensify. Her body was now soft and pliant as he held her, and there was more curiosity than fear in her brown gaze.

Curiosity and a glimmer of feminine heat.

The realization that she wanted him—and the intoxicating scent of her growing arousal—made his groin tighten. The balmy air inside their shelter suddenly felt steaming hot, and his skin prickled as her hands shifted on his chest, her palms splaying on his skin without any attempt to push him away.

She licked her lips again, her eyes darkening, and Arus could no longer control himself.

Sliding his hand into her hair, he lowered his head and claimed that tempting mouth with a kiss.

CHAPTER FIVE

Caught in the god's powerful embrace, Delia felt like she'd been swept up by the storm. When Arus had first picked her up, she'd been too anxious to focus on his naked body, but as her fear abated, the unfamiliar ache between her thighs returned—and with it, an intense awareness of him as an attractive man.

A man who wanted her, judging by the large erection pressing against her bottom.

Delia was a virgin, but she wasn't ignorant about the mechanics of sex. She'd watched many animals mate, and her mother had told her it was the same for humans. Delia also knew she shouldn't mate with anyone but her husband. It was a rule she had always intended to follow—except it now seemed that her husband was likely to be Phanias. She couldn't imagine so much as kissing the old blacksmith, and the idea of this exotic, powerful stranger taking her virginity was more than a little appealing.

So appealing, in fact, that when Arus lowered his head to kiss her, she pushed her fear of him aside and let herself simply feel.

His lips were surprisingly soft as they touched her own, and his breath was warm and faintly sweet, like he'd recently eaten a piece of fruit. His tongue probed at the seam of her lips, and she parted them instinctively. He immediately took advantage, his tongue sweeping into her mouth as his hand tightened in her hair, and the ache inside her core intensified, transforming into a peculiar pulsing tension. Her breasts felt full and sensitive, her nipples peaking as if from being rubbed, and a liquid warmth gathered between her thighs as he deepened the kiss, all but devouring her with his tongue.

He tasted both sweet and slightly salty, as if some sea water lingered on his lips. Delia's head fell back, giving in to the pressure of his mouth, and she moaned, her hands sliding up to grip his strong shoulders. The heat inside her grew as he shifted underneath her, his arms tightening around her body. His erection was like an iron rod under her bottom, and the knowledge that he desired her so much both thrilled and terrified her.

She'd heard the first time always hurt, and she wasn't looking forward to the pain.

Still, even that worry wasn't enough to cool the fire under her skin. Everything within her craved Arus's touch. The need for him consumed her, making her feel like a stranger in her own body. For the first time, Delia understood why Helen of Troy risked everything for Paris.

If this was passion, no wonder wars were fought over it.

Before Delia had a chance to dwell on that, Arus lowered her to the ground, stretching her out on the still-damp grass. She managed to tear her mouth away from him long enough to gulp in a much-needed breath, and then he was on top of her, his large body blocking out her view of the storm raging outside. She still didn't understand how a transparent wall could protect them from rain and lightning, but as he resumed kissing her, she lost all inclination to care.

Whatever magic powers the god possessed paled next to the desire he evoked in her.

His hands were now traveling over her body, big, strong, and determined. There was skill and experience in his touch. He didn't grab at her breasts like the boy who'd kissed her when she was sixteen; instead, Arus kneaded her small mounds through her dress, his thumb flicking back and forth over her hardened nipples as he held himself up on his elbows. At the same time, his knee parted her legs, wedging between them, and she felt his thigh press against her sex, putting pressure on a spot that made her feel hot and dizzy. The pulsing ache within her intensified, and she gasped into his mouth, her hands clutching at his sides as the tension in her core coiled tighter and tighter.

"Yes, that's it," he whispered, moving his lips to Delia's ear. "Come for me, darling." His thigh moved rhythmically between her legs, rubbing against her sex through the rough material of her dress, and the tension inside her worsened. She could feel the heat of his breath on her neck, and her heartbeat thundered in her ears, her vision dimming as a throbbing pressure built inside her. It felt like she was dying, like something within her was about to explode. Frightened, she cried out the god's name—and then the explosion was upon her.

Every bit of pressure that built up seemed to release at the same time, sending intense pleasure blasting out from her core. Her inner muscles spasmed repeatedly, and her toes curled. Gasping, Delia lifted her hips, seeking more of the sensations, but the pleasure was already ebbing, leaving her dazed and breathless.

Before she could understand what had happened, Arus rolled off her, stood up, and pulled her to her feet. She stood, swaying on unsteady legs, as he pulled her dress over her head and dropped it on the ground, leaving her naked—and starkly aware of the large, aroused male standing in front of her.

"Wait," she whispered, but he was already bearing her down to the ground and covering her with his powerful body. There were no barriers between them now, and Delia's earlier fear returned as she felt the insistent hardness of his erection against her leg. Her heartbeat spiking, she wedged her hands between them, her palms pushing at his chest.

"Don't be afraid," he murmured, holding himself up on one elbow. He slid his free hand down her body in a soothing caress, and she saw that his eyes were as dark as a midnight sky, his beautiful features tightly drawn. "I won't hurt you," he promised roughly, spreading her thighs open with his knees.

Delia opened her mouth to tell him she was a virgin, but he was already touching her sex, his fingers unerringly finding the spot that made her so tense before. It was even more sensitive now, and she could feel a strange, warm slickness inside her. Embarrassed, she tried to move away before he could feel her wetness, but his fingers were already there, parting her folds and pushing into her body.

It was just the tips of his two fingers, but Delia flinched away, the stretching sensation both unfamiliar and painful. Instantly, Arus stopped, looking down at her.

"What is it?" He sounded worried.

"I—" Delia felt her face heat up with a flush. "I haven't done this before."

His eyes widened, and for a brief moment, she thought he would release her. However, in the next second, his jaw tightened, and she saw a muscle pulsing near his ear. "Never?" he asked hoarsely, and Delia shook her head, too embarrassed to say it again.

He stared at her, his gaze oddly intent, and she realized that his hand was still on her sex, his fingers poised at the entrance to her body. "So you're all mine." There was a darkly possessive note in his voice. "No man has ever touched you."

Delia bit her lip. "Not—" She gasped as he pushed one finger into her. "Not like this."

His nostrils flared, and then he was kissing her again, his mouth consuming her with savage hunger as his finger pressed deeper into her. The sensation was foreign, but not painful, and the now-familiar tension returned as his thumb found the sensitive spot from before. The slickness inside her eased the path for his finger, and after a moment, Delia forgot all about her initial discomfort, her hips rocking to the movements of his hand.

Maybe she got lucky, and her first time wouldn't hurt at all.

CHAPTER SIX

Delia's pussy was so tight around his finger Arus knew he was going to end up hurting her. The only way to avoid that would be to stop and leave her alone, but that was beyond his capabilities. The lust riding him was dark and visceral, more potent than anything he'd ever experienced.

He wanted to possess this human girl, to claim her in every way possible.

The primitive desire stunned him, but he couldn't analyze it at the moment. His skin was burning, and his cock was so hard it hurt. He needed to be inside her, to feel her tight, wet flesh rippling around him.

Her mouth was warm and sweet as he devoured her with his kiss, and the scent of her drove him insane.

He had to fuck her. Now.

Calling on every bit of his remaining self-control, Arus used his thumb to bring her to another orgasm, wanting her to be as wet and ready as possible. She cried out, her inner muscles contracting around his finger, and he used the opportunity to press a second finger into her narrow channel, preparing her for his possession. She stiffened under him, flinching despite her wetness, and he knew there was no way to avoid causing her some pain.

Raising his head, he pulled his hand away, grabbed his cock, and aligned it with her pussy. "I'm sorry," he whispered, catching her pleasure-dazed gaze, and before she could respond, he began to push in.

Delia cried out, pushing at his chest, but Arus persisted, knowing he had to breach her hymen. Her inner moisture helped, but she was still incredibly tight, her body tensing to resist his penetration. He lowered his head, raining kisses over her face and whispering that it was going to be all right, that the pain would ease soon, but he could see his reassurances weren't helping. She let out a pained cry as he pressed deeper, and despite his balls getting ready to explode, he paused as he felt the wetness on her cheeks.

He wanted her, but he hated causing her pain.

"Do you want me to stop?" he forced himself to ask, even though everything within him rebelled at the notion. His cock was only halfway inside her, and if he was already hurting her this much . . .

Delia stilled, staring up at him with tear-filled brown eyes, and he saw that she was breathing erratically, her chest heaving as her delicate hands pressed against his chest, as if trying to hold him at bay.

"Do you want me to stop?" Arus repeated, ignoring the pounding of blood in his temples. Despite the primal need gnawing at his insides, he was not a savage. He'd lived over two hundred years without fucking this girl, and he could survive it if she made him wait.

He hoped so, at least.

To his tremendous relief, she moved her head in a small, uncertain shake. "No," she whispered, blinking rapidly. "It just—"

Arus didn't have a chance to hear what she had to say because the last remaining thread of his restraint snapped. Leaning down, he took her lips in a deep, carnal kiss and pushed forward in one merciless stroke, tearing through the thin membrane blocking his way.

Tight, wet heat engulfed him, her flesh squeezing him like a fist, and Arus's spine bowed as sharp, stunning pleasure rocketed through him, sending his heartbeat spiking. She was beyond delicious, beyond perfect. It was as if her slim body had been made just for him. He felt lost in her, consumed by the sensations, but before he could get completely carried away, he tasted something salty on his lips.

Her tears.

They stopped him cold.

Raising his head to gaze down at her, Arus forced himself to hold still and not thrust. She was shaking, her face streaked with tears, and he knew he had to give her time to get used to him, to adjust to the invasion of her body. He managed to control himself for a few brief moments—and then the metallic scent of her virgin's blood reached his nostrils.

A dark, ancient hunger roared to life within him, mingling with his lust and intensifying it. The pull of predatory instinct was impossible to resist. Groaning, Arus lowered his face to her neck and felt her pulse beating under his lips. Delia was breathing fast, still trying to cope with the pain of her lost virginity, but her body was no longer the only thing Arus needed.

Opening his mouth, he sliced the sharp edges of his teeth across her tender skin.

Her blood spurted onto his tongue. Hot, rich, and coppery, it was an aphrodisiac a thousand times stronger than the synthetic versions on Krina. Genetic modification had ensured his people were no longer reliant on blood to survive, but the craving for the resulting high had never gone away. Arus could hear Delia crying out, feel her nails digging into his skin, and he realized distantly that the pacifying chemical in his saliva was working on her—that she was feeling some of the mind-bending pleasure that held him in its grip.

That was his last coherent thought. Everything afterwards was a blur of violent ecstasy, of her taste and scent and feel. Arus took the girl relentlessly, without restraint, and she met his savage thrusts with equal hunger, her slender limbs wrapped around him as he fucked her for hours on end. The bliss rushing through his veins left him unable to think or reason; all he knew was that he had to have her, over and over again.

When he finally rolled off her limp body, spent and sated, the sky above their shelter was dark and clear. He could see the stars, and he knew the storm had passed.

It was safe to let her go now, except he didn't want to.

Arus wanted to keep Delia for the rest of his life.

CHAPTER SEVEN

Delia woke up gradually, the images from her dream lingering in her mind as she slowly returned to consciousness. Her eyes still closed, she smiled, thinking how she'd never had such a sublime dream before. Even now, her sex throbbed pleasantly from the memory of the god's possession—of his powerful body driving into her as she lost herself in the heated rapture of his embrace.

There had been pain too, she recalled, but it had been over with quickly. She'd felt torn in half when Arus had first entered her, but then he had done something—touched her neck in a way that had initially stung—and the pain had dissolved, replaced by unimaginable ecstasy.

By a sexual pleasure so intense just the thought of it made her insides clench.

Still smiling, Delia rolled over, reluctant to wake up fully. It was incredible how vivid her dream had been. The storm, the bubble-like shelter made of transparent walls, even the god's unusual name— she'd never been able to remember so many details from her other dreams.

This dream had felt real. So real, in fact, that she could still smell the clean male scent of Arus's skin and feel his hand stroking her hair.

Wait a minute. There *was* a hand stroking her hair.

Delia bolted upright, her eyes flying open, and she saw him: the god she'd just been dreaming about.

Except it hadn't been a dream—it couldn't have been, because she wasn't in her family's ramshackle hut.

She was on a strange bed in a room with ivory walls, and she was naked in front of Arus, who was sitting next to her dressed in an odd-looking white outfit.

Gasping, Delia grabbed for the nearest piece of cloth—a sheet that felt incredibly soft as she wrapped it around herself. Her heart racing, she jumped off the bed and gaped at the god, who was regarding her with an unreadable expression on his beautiful face.

"Where am I?" Delia's voice shook as she cast a frantic glance around the room. "What is this place?"

Everything around her was ivory-colored, and there were no windows or doors. And the bed— No, surely her eyes were deceiving her.

The bed, which was just a flat white board, was floating in mid-air.

"You're on my ship," Arus said, getting off the board to walk toward her. His dark eyes gleamed as he stopped in front of her, causing her to crane her neck to look up at him. "I brought you here so I could make sure you weren't sore after last night."

Delia must've looked as uncomprehending as she felt, because he explained, "We have healing technology here."

"Oh." Overwhelmed, Delia stared up at him. Now that he'd pointed it out, she realized there wasn't even the slightest soreness between her legs. Details from last night continued to return to her, and she remembered how painful the initial breaching of her maidenhead had been—and how he'd kept thrusting into her afterwards for what must've been hours.

By all rights, she should've been *very* sore.

"You healed me?"

"I did." Raising his hand, Arus cupped her jaw with his large palm, his thumb stroking gently over her cheek. "I didn't want you to be in pain."

"Oh." Delia exhaled, everything inside her reacting to that warm, comforting touch. She didn't know what to do, how to respond to his peculiar kindness, so finally she just said, "Thank you."

Arus's chiseled lips curved in a smile. "You're welcome, darling. Now, are you hungry?"

Delia's stomach chose that moment to rumble, and he laughed. "Sounds like you are."

* * *

He fed her food that tasted like ambrosia—a mixture of some unfamiliar fruits, vegetables, and nuts, with a sauce that made Delia's taste buds weep with pleasure. He got the food directly from one of the walls. It had parted at his command, delivering the bounty they were feasting on while sitting at a floating table—which had also come out of a wall.

"What kind of ship is this?" Delia asked when she was full. She didn't understand Arus's magic, but it didn't terrify her quite as much anymore. It was clear to her that he didn't intend her any harm—and that he had to have come from Mount Olympus, despite his earlier protestations.

"It's a ship that carries us between distant worlds," Arus said, and his answer solidified her conviction. "The stars you see are not just little lights in the sky; they're suns, like the one giving Earth heat and light. Those suns have planets like Earth orbiting around them, and I come from one of those planets." He paused, waiting for her questions, but Delia had no idea where to begin.

All she got from his explanation was that his ship had carried him here from the stars—which meant that Mount Olympus was a place in the sky, rather than the mountain of legend.

Arus sighed, looking at her. "You don't understand, do you?" A rueful smile tugged at the corner of his beautiful mouth. "I guess I should've expected that. I wish I could convince you that none of this is supernatural, that we're just a more advanced civilization, but you'd have to learn a great deal before that would make sense to you. So for now, if it helps you to think of me as a god, you may do so."

Delia smiled, oddly reassured by his words. "You *are* a god. What else could you possibly be?"

"I'm a Krinar," he said, and she saw his face assume a more serious expression. "Delia," he said quietly, "there's something I'd like to ask you."

She blinked. "What is it?"

"I have to leave soon. To go home to Krina."

Her chest squeezed painfully at his words. "Of course," she managed to say. "You said it's beautiful there, and you have to return."

Arus nodded. "I do—and I would like you to come with me." Before she could do more than gape at him, he said, "I know I'm still a stranger to you, and that everything about this"—he swept his hand out in a wide arc—"must seem foreign and frightening. But I promise I won't hurt you, and I'll take care of you. You'll be safe with me."

Delia couldn't believe her ears. "You want me to come with you? To the world where you live?"

"Yes, to Krina—or Mount Olympus, or whatever you want to call it." Arus reached across the floating table and took her hand. "It *is* a beautiful place, and if you come with me, I can promise you a life beyond anything you can imagine."

Delia had to be still dreaming. "Why?" she said in disbelief. "Why would you take me with you?"

Arus rose to his feet and pulled her up with him, his gaze filling with carnal heat as he stepped around the table. "Because our time together wasn't nearly enough for me," he said, drawing her against his hard, aroused body. "Because I had you, and I want more—so much more. I want you to be mine, so I can have you every day and every night for a long, long time."

Delia's pulse was rabbit fast, and a million questions crowded her mind as Arus gazed down at her, his erection pushing against her belly. His blunt declaration was far from tender words of love, and there were so many things she didn't know about him and the world he wanted to take her to. But he was giving her a choice, and that fact alone helped quell her fear.

She could stay and live an ordinary life—most likely as the blacksmith's wife—or she could follow this gorgeous stranger to a mysterious place in the sky.

"What about my family?" she asked as the thought occurred to her. "They need the mussels and I—"

"I'll leave them your weight in gold before we go," Arus said. "They won't lack for anything ever again."

"But—"

"Come with me, Delia." Arus's eyes glittered as his arms tightened around her back. "Your family will be fine, I promise. Come with me, and let me show you the wonders of my world."

She stared at his magnificent features, remembering how he'd saved her from the storm—how he'd sheltered her, fed her, healed her, and given her more pleasure than she'd ever thought possible. He was right: her family would be fine without her—better off, in fact. Even without the gold, she was an extra mouth to feed. And if Arus truly gave them that much wealth, her sisters would have their pick of suitors instead of being forced to marry out of desperation.

It was that last thought that solidified her decision. Delia had no idea what would happen to her if she came with him, what his world was like or how they could travel to the stars, but at that moment, caught in her god's embrace, she knew she wanted to find out.

It was unthinkable, insane, deliriously frightening, but Delia took a leap into the unknown and said, "Yes, Arus. I'll come with you."

ADDITIONAL READING

Thank you for reading this story! I hope you enjoyed it. If you'd like to see more of Arus & Delia and learn about the Krinar, you can pick up *The Krinar Chronicles*, a trilogy of three full-length novels featuring another human-Krinar couple—Mia & Korum. M&K's story takes place in modern times, a few years after the Krinar invasion. Alternatively, if you liked this story but prefer contemporary romance, you're welcome to check out my dark erotic trilogy, *Twist Me*.

Please visit my website at www.annazaires.com to sign up for my new release email list and to learn more about my upcoming books.

Close Liaisons by Anna Zaires

A dark and edgy romance that will appeal to fans of erotic and turbulent relationships . . .

In the near future, the Krinar rule the Earth. An advanced race from another galaxy, they are still a mystery to us—and we are completely at their mercy.

Shy and innocent, Mia Stalis is a college student in New York City who has led a very normal life. Like most people, she's never had any interactions with the invaders—until one fateful day in the park changes everything. Having caught Korum's eye, she must now contend with a powerful, dangerously seductive Krinar who wants to possess her and will stop at nothing to make her his own.

How far would you go to regain your freedom? How much would you sacrifice to help your people? What choice will you make when you begin to fall for your enemy?

If you're more interested in contemporary romance, you might like my dark erotic series *Twist Me*. It's also available at most retailers.

Twist Me by Anna Zaires

Kidnapped. Taken to a private island.

I never thought this could happen to me. I never imagined one chance meeting on the eve of my eighteenth birthday could change my life so completely.

Now I belong to him. To Julian. To a man who is as ruthless as he is beautiful—a man whose touch makes me burn. A man whose tenderness I find more devastating than his cruelty.

My captor is an enigma. I don't know who he is or why he took me. There is a darkness inside him—a darkness that scares me even as it draws me in.

My name is Nora Leston, and this is my story.

For fantasy/sci-fi fans among you, I encourage you to check out *The Thought Readers*, the first book in the *Mind Dimensions* series. It's my collaboration with Dima Zales, my husband. But please be warned, there's not much romance or sex in this one. Instead of sex, there's mind reading. The book can be ordered at most retailers.

The Thought Readers by **Dima Zales**

Everyone thinks I'm a genius.

Everyone is wrong.

Sure, I finished Harvard at eighteen and now make crazy money at a hedge fund. But that's not because I'm unusually smart or hard-working.

It's because I cheat.

You see, I have a unique ability. I can go outside time into my own personal version of reality—the place I call "the Quiet"—where I can explore my surroundings while the rest of the world stands still.

I thought I was the only one who could do this—until I met her.

My name is Darren, and this is how I learned that I'm a Reader.

* * *

For additional purchase links, audiobook links, foreign translations, and more, please visit www.annazaires.com.

ABOUT THE AUTHOR

Anna Zaires is a *New York Times*, *USA Today*, and international bestselling author of sci-fi romance and contemporary dark erotic romance. She fell in love with books at the age of five, when her grandmother taught her to read. Since then, she has always lived partially in a fantasy world where the only limits were those of her imagination. Currently residing in Florida, Anna is happily married to Dima Zales (a science fiction and fantasy author) and closely collaborates with him on all their works.

Please visit www.annazaires.com to learn more.